Copyright © 1995 by Nord-Süd Verlag AG, Gossau Zürich, Switzerland
First published in Switzerland under the title *Hoppel lernt Schwimmen.*
English translation copyright © 1995 by North-South Books Inc.

First published in the United States, Great Britain, Canada,
Australia, and New Zealand in 1995 by North-South Books,
an imprint of Nord-Süd Verlag AG, Gossau Zürich, Switzerland.
First paperback edition published in 1997.

Library of Congress Cataloging-in-Publication Data
[Hoppel lernt schwimmen. English]
Hang on, Hopper! / by Marcus Pfister : translated by Rosemary Lanning.
Summary: Hopper the Arctic hare attempts a shortcut across a river even though he cannot swim.
[1, Hares—Fiction. 2. Rabbits—Fiction.] I. Lanning, Rosemary. II. Title.
PZ7.P448558Hag 1995 [E]—dc-20 94-43635

A CIP catalogue record for this book is available from The British Library.

ISBN 1-55858-403-X (trade binding)
3 5 7 9 TB 10 8 6 4 2
ISBN 1-55858-404-8 (library binding)
3 5 7 9 LB 10 8 6 4 2
ISBN 1-55858-771-3 (paperback)
1 3 5 7 9 PB 10 8 6 4 2
Printed in Belgium

For more information about our books, and the authors and artists
who create them, visit our web site: http://www.northsouth.com

Hang On, Hopper!

By Marcus Pfister

TRANSLATED BY ROSEMARY LANNING

North-South Books / New York / London

Spring had finally come to the high plains. Feeling restless, Hopper said to his mother, "Now that the snow has melted, may I go down into the valley and play with my friend Scamp?"

"Of course you may," she said. "But remember how far it is, and make sure you get home before dark."

"I will, Mama," said the little arctic hare, and off he ran.

The forest where Scamp lived was a wonderful place for games of hide-and-seek, and the two young hares played happily all afternoon.

Suddenly Hopper realized how late it was. "Oh no!" he said. "I promised I'd be home before dark."

"Don't worry," said Scamp. "I know a short-cut across the river."

"But I can't swim," said Hopper.

"Anyone can swim," said his friend. "It's easy!"

Hopper nervously dipped a paw in the river. "Are you sure I can do this?" he asked. "The water is very cold."

"You're just scared!" said Scamp. "I'm not. Watch me!" and he boldly jumped in.

Hopper lowered himself into the river and pushed off from the bank.

At once he disappeared under the water; then he bobbed back up again, coughing and sputtering.

"Help!" he gasped, swallowing another mouthful of water.

Hopper felt the current pulling him. He was sure he was going to drown.

"Grab that piece of wood!" called Scamp.

Hopper managed to splash over to a wooden plank that was floating in the river. He clung tightly to the plank and saw Scamp running along the riverbank. But the current grew so strong that Scamp could not keep up. As he watched his friend disappear around a bend, he shouted out, "Hang on, Hopper!"

Slowly the current grew weaker, and the river opened into a small pond. Hopper was washed up against an island of twigs and branches. He clambered out of the water and shook himself dry.

"Hey! Watch where you're stepping! That's my house," said a deep voice behind him. Hopper turned and found himself face-to-face with a beaver.

"How did you get here?" asked the beaver, and Hopper told him everything that had happened. "That short-cut was a big mistake," said the beaver. "Water is dangerous. Stay away from it if you can't swim."

"I will," said Hopper, looking rather ashamed of himself. "And I'm sorry I stepped on your house. I didn't know it *was* a house. There is no door."

"Oh yes there is," said the beaver. He slid into the water, twisted, turned, and disappeared under the pile of sticks.

"That was good," said Hopper when the beaver came back. "When winter comes, I'm going to build myself a house like this, with a secret door under the snow." Then he looked anxious. "I should be at home now," he said. "Mother will be worried about me. How can I get back across the water?"

"I'll help you," said the beaver. "Just climb on my back."

Hopper held on tight as the beaver swam strongly across the pond. The beaver set him down gently on the riverbank. "Off you go, little hare," he said kindly. "Come back another day and I'll give you swimming lessons."

"Hopper!" his mother was calling from the edge of the forest. Scamp had run to get her, and they had been searching for Hopper all along the river.

Hopper was so happy to see her that he forgot how scared he had been. "I was swimming, Mama," he said proudly. "You should have seen me."

Scamp had been even more frightened than Hopper. "I'm very sorry," he said to Hopper's mother. "It was my fault for making Hopper take that short-cut. But please, will you let him stay with me tonight, so we can play again tomorrow?"

"Only if you promise that there will be no more short-cuts," said Hopper's mother with a smile.

It was already dark when the two little hares reached Scamp's home. His mother was waiting anxiously for him, knowing what trouble Scamp could get into. When they told her all about their day, she smiled but shook her head. "Tomorrow you must both stay close by me," she said. "No more swimming for either of you."

Then, with Scamp's mother watching over them, the two best friends snuggled down together and went to sleep.